SUNNY and the HOTEL SPLENDID

ALISON MOORE has been writing stories since she was a child, and was first published – through a local writing competition – when she was eight. She began writing her first novel, *The Lighthouse*, the year her son was born, and recently published her fourth novel and her first book for children, *Sunny and the Ghosts*. She lives in a village on the Leicestershire-Nottinghamshire border with her husband and son and a cat called Shadow.

ROSS COLLINS was born in Glasgow, Scotland, quite a while ago. At that time he would eat anything and resembled a currant bun. Ross has written sixteen children's books and illustrated over a hundred. He no longer resembles a currant bun. He lives in Glasgow with a strange woman, a small child and a stupid dog.

SUNNY and the HOTEL SPLENDID

Alison Moore

Illustrated by Ross Collins

SALT

CROMER

PUBLISHED BY SALT PUBLISHING 2019

2 4 6 8 10 9 7 5 3 1

Copyright © Alison Moore 2019

First published in Great Britain in 2019 by
Salt Publishing Ltd
12 Norwich Road, Cromer, Norfolk NR27 0AX United Kingdom

www.saltpublishing.com

Salt Publishing Limited Reg. No. 5293401

A CIP catalogue record for this book is available from the British Library

ISBN 978 1 78463 202 1 (Paperback edition)
ISBN 978 1 78463 203 8 (Electronic edition)

Typeset in Neacademia by Salt Publishing

Printed and bound in Great Britain by Clays Ltd, Elcograf S.p.A

For Arthur, Douglas and Penny

Sometimes, a sound in an empty room is just a breeze coming in through an open window, billowing a curtain, toppling a vase, scattering some papers, slamming a door. And sometimes it's not.

CHAPTER ONE

The Hotel

I T WAS THE end of July, and nearly teatime. It had been the hottest day of the year so far and the beach was still packed with holidaymakers playing in the sand and in the sea. Most of the hotels along the seafront were full. They had signs in their front windows to let people know that there were no empty rooms – the signs said 'NO VACANCIES'.

Along the promenade came Ana and her mum. Ana's suitcase-on-wheels trundled noisily behind her, while her shadow followed silently. Her mum came to a stop outside a hotel whose sign said 'VACANCIES', and Ana asked, 'Is this where we're staying?'

'I think so,' said her mum, squinting up at the letters that spelt out the name of the hotel. Some of the letters were missing. The Hotel Splendid was a fine old building but it looked a bit unloved. 'It's a bit dilapidated,' said Ana's mum. 'It could do with a fresh coat of paint and a new sign.'

They headed for the entrance, and Ana said, 'I like it.'

Ana's mum opened the door into the foyer. They could see that it must have been grand in its heyday, but now the wallpaper was faded and the carpet was threadbare. There was no one behind the little reception desk to welcome them.

On the desk, next to a display of postcards, there was a bell which could be rung so that someone would know they were there. Ana asked if she could ring it, and although her mum was first into the foyer, she said yes, Ana could ring it.

As Ana was making her way through the doorway, her suitcase got stuck. She had turned around to see what the problem was when she heard the bell on the reception desk ding.

'I thought you said I could ring the bell,' said Ana, freeing her suitcase and wheeling it into the foyer.

'I did,' said her mum, sounding puzzled.

Behind the reception desk, a door marked 'PRIVATE' opened and a woman emerged wearing a sequined top that caught the light like a glitter ball. She came to the desk and said, 'Yes?'

Ana's mum was looking at the bell.

'You rang the bell?' said the woman.

'No,' said Ana's mum. 'It rang all by itself.'

The woman looked at the bell. She dinged it, as if to make the point that it did not ring all by itself.

Ana's mum said, 'I booked a room. The name's Sharma.'

'I'm Mrs Griffin,' said the woman. 'Welcome to the Hotel Splendid.' While Mrs Griffin was looking at her computer screen, tapping on her keyboard and scrolling with her mouse, saying, 'Sometimes I think this computer has a mind of its own,' Ana and her mum were looking around the foyer.

On one side of the reception desk, there was a potted palm tree as tall as Mrs Griffin. Ana's mum admired it, and Mrs Griffin said that she hardly ever remembered to water it but that it seemed to thrive nonetheless.

On the other side of the reception desk was what looked like a piano, but it was not quite like the piano that was played when they sang in assembly at Ana's school – Mrs Griffin's instrument was more ornate, with a row of knobs above the keyboard, and big pedals. Ana's mum said it was splendid. 'Unfortunately,' said Mrs Griffin, 'it doesn't seem to work. I can't get a sound out of it. Such a shame.' She looked at her computer screen and sighed.

'I expect you're very busy,' said Ana's mum, 'in Devon at the height of the holiday season.'

'Actually,' said Mrs Griffin, 'you're the only customers I've got booked in all week.'

Ana's mum noticed the keys hanging from numbered hooks behind the reception desk. They were all there except for the key that belonged on hook number one. Reaching for the key on the very last hook, Mrs Griffin said, 'Your room is ready.'

'You do have *someone* else staying,' said Ana's mum, 'in room one?'

'Oh,' said Mrs Griffin, 'no, there's no one in that room. I've lost the key. I lost it months ago and can't think where it's got to.' She stepped out from behind the reception desk. 'Please follow me. Just mind the wobbly post at the bottom of the stairs. There's always something that needs fixing in an old building like this. Oh, this door . . .' In the triangle of space beneath the stairs, there was a cupboard whose door was ajar. 'It won't stay shut.' Ana could see a stepladder and tools and paint and so on, organised on shelves and hooks inside the cupboard. Mrs Griffin closed the cupboard door, picked up Ana's suitcase and set off up the stairs. 'It's quite a climb, I'm afraid,' she said. 'I've put you in an attic room.'

Ana wondered why, if they were the only guests, they had been put all the way up in the attic, right at the top of the hotel. She supposed the view was better from there.

The first flight of stairs brought them to one end of a long corridor with rooms – closed doors – on either side. As they turned to set off up the next flight of stairs to the second floor, they heard a noise that seemed to come from one of the nearby first-floor rooms. It was a crashing, smashing noise.

'Don't worry about that noise,' said Mrs Griffin as they climbed. 'There's no one in those rooms. I don't think you'll be disturbed during your stay – your room is right at the top of the hotel – but if you do hear any strange noises, please don't let them worry you.'

'Noises?' said Ana's mum.

'Like the one we just heard?' asked Ana.

'Don't let them worry you,' repeated Mrs Griffin, hurrying on up the stairs.

Outside their attic room, Mrs Griffin apologised for a patch of water damage on the ceiling. 'The leak has been dealt with,' she said, 'but I'm afraid the stain is rather unsightly.' She unlocked the door and ushered Ana and her mum inside. She showed them where everything was, including the sea view. She told them what time they should come down for breakfast, and gave them their room key. 'If you need anything, just ask,' she said. 'I'm always here.'

Mrs Griffin left the room, and Ana had a look around. There were two beds and she tested them both to make sure they were nice and bouncy. On the bed nearest the window, she put her cuddly toys. On the bedside table, she put her book of ghost stories. She believed in ghosts, even though she had never seen one. She had begged her mum to take her to haunted houses and haunted castles. Her mum – who did not believe in ghosts but who liked exploring interesting places – had taken her to Berry Pomeroy Castle, where a ghost was said to haunt the tower and the dungeons, but Ana had not seen it. They had been to Compton Castle, where a ghost in seventeenth-century clothes was sometimes glimpsed at dusk, but Ana had not seen it. They had been to Okehampton Castle, reputedly haunted by the ghost of a wicked lady and a spectral black dog, but Ana had not seen them. They had been to all these places and more, but in none of them had Ana seen a ghost. She still loved reading stories about ghosts, but she was starting to think that she might never see a real one, and that, in fact, they might not be real after all.

Ana unpacked her suitcase and looked through the window at the beach below. She was looking forward to walking barefoot on the sand and having fish and chips and ice cream for tea. She said to her mum, 'Can we go to the beach now?'

Her mum hung the last of her things in the ward-robe and put away the empty suitcases. 'Yes,' she said. 'Let's go and explore.'

They left the room and made their way down-stairs. When they reached the first floor, as they turned to go down the last flight of stairs, Ana paused.

'What is it?' asked her mum.

'I'm just listening,' said Ana.

'Listening to what?' asked her mum.

'I'm listening for noises,' said Ana, 'but I can't hear anything.'

Her mum listened too, but there was nothing to hear now, and they continued on their way down the stairs to the ground floor.

It was deathly quiet in the foyer. There was no one behind the reception desk. Ana skipped ahead, over the thinning carpet, towards the front door. When she heard the bell on the reception desk ding, she turned around. Her mum was a few steps from the desk, walking away from it towards Ana, turning her head, too, to look at the bell.

Mrs Griffin came through the door behind the desk and said, 'Yes?'

Ana's mum looked at her, perplexed.

'I heard the bell,' said Mrs Griffin.

'But I didn't ring it,' said Ana's mum.

Mrs Griffin looked at Ana.

'I didn't ring it either,' said Ana.

'Well somebody did,' said Mrs Griffin. She looked around, as if to make the point that there was clearly no one else there who might have done it.

Ana and her mum headed outside. As they left the

cool foyer, Ana's mum whispered, 'It's a very strange place.'

Ana glanced back at the shabby hotel. 'I like it,' she said. With the salty sea smell in her nostrils and sunshine on her arms and legs, she skipped along the promenade, and her shadow skipped along with her.

CHAPTER TWO

The Postcard

SOME MILES INLAND, in a flat above a shop, Sunny and his mum and dad were eating beans on toast for their tea. It was the first day of the school summer holidays, and Sunny had spent it helping out in the shop. The shop sold things that were antique, vintage, second-hand – things that were old. Sunny's job was to help fix whatever was broken, and to polish whatever was dusty or dull. He loved the shop and all the old things in it, but all day long the sun had been shining through the display windows and he had found himself wishing that he were at the seaside instead, running along a sandy seashore, dashing into and out of the water.

'I'll be out and about tomorrow,' said Sunny's dad. 'I need to deliver something . . .' He took a piece of paper out of his pocket, unfolded it and looked at the name at the top. '. . . to the Hotel Splendid.'

Sunny and his mum said at the same time, 'The Hotel Splendid?'

'We got a postcard from there this morning,' said Sunny's mum.

'We did?' said Sunny.

'Yes,' said his mum, finding and showing him the postcard with a picture of the Hotel Splendid on the front. It was addressed to *Everyone*, at the shop's address. *I wonder*, the neat handwriting on the postcard said, *if you might have time to come and visit us. We love being here but sometimes we feel a bit lonely. With love from Mary and Elsie.*

'It's from Mary and Elsie!' said Sunny.

'Yes,' said his mum, 'but who *are* Mary and Elsie?'

'Mary and Elsie from London,' said Sunny.

His mum pulled a trying-to-think face.

'The twin sisters,' said Sunny.

His mum pulled a trying-*really*-hard-to-remember face.

'The ghosts,' said Sunny.

'Ah,' said his mum. 'The ghosts.'

Sometimes, the antique, vintage and second-hand goods that arrived in the shop came with ghosts, although Sunny's mum and dad could not see them. There were currently four ghosts downstairs, and Mary and Elsie had stayed there briefly before deciding to move to the seaside. Sunny was glad Mary and Elsie liked their new home but he did not like to think of them feeling lonely.

'Do you think we could *all* go?' asked Sunny. 'For a day trip, like we did on my birthday?'

'That was a lovely day,' said his mum.

'How about,' said his dad, 'we close the shop for the week and have a holiday. Shall I see if this hotel can squeeze us in?'

'That would be brilliant,' said Sunny. He finished his tea while his dad made the phone call, and when his dad came back into the kitchen to say, 'We're in luck!' Sunny picked up the postcard and headed for the stairs, calling back over his shoulder, 'I'll go and tell the ghosts!'

Downstairs, everything was quiet. The ghosts found it very uncomfortable when people walked through them or sat where they were sitting, so they tended to hide themselves away during daylight hours, only coming out when everyone else went to bed.

Sunny opened the lid of the blanket box, inside which Herbert had been thinking about a tune that he was composing, for playing on the piano.

Sunny let Violet out of the stationery cupboard, where she spent her days coming up with ideas for the stories that she wrote at night.

He opened the door of Walter's wardrobe. Walter would be kept busy all night helping Herbert with his composition, and helping Violet by reading and editing her stories, and talking to Abigail.

Abigail had arrived in the shop inside another, fancier wardrobe. It had curlicues and a mirrored door and was a very fine piece of furniture, but she preferred to be out socialising. Even Abigail hid herself away during the day though, ever since her bus-stop experience. She had been chatting away to a queue of people when the bus arrived and everyone getting off the bus had walked through her; then, before she had quite recovered, the people who had been queueing went through her to get onto the bus. She was staggering back to the shop when a young man riding his bicycle on the pavement went through her at speed. Now, Abigail, like the rest of the ghosts, spent most of the daylight hours in a safe place inside the shop.

At night, Abigail sat and talked to Herbert, unless Herbert wanted to read; or she talked to Violet, but when Violet was trying to concentrate on her work she liked a bit of peace and quiet; or she talked to Walter, until he got tired and was ready to go back inside his wardrobe. She liked to talk a lot. She talked to Sunny if he came down to the shop before bed or in the early hours, and sometimes she talked to Sunny's parents while they were getting ready to open the shop in the morning, but because they could neither see nor hear her, they did not respond.

Abigail liked to talk about her years in the theatre, telling stories about plays she had been in and actors she had worked with, although the truth was that she had only ever been in crowd scenes. She had always wanted a starring role but had never been given one. On a few occasions, she had been an understudy, learning a role in case the person playing that part was ill or for some other reason was unable to go on stage, but she had never been needed.

When Sunny had got all the ghosts gathered together, he showed them the postcard that Mary and Elsie had sent and told them that the shop was going to close for the week so that they could go to the seaside. 'We can stay at the Hotel Splendid,' he said, 'and see Mary and Elsie. Do you all want to come?'

'I do!' said Violet. 'It would be lovely to see them again. Also, I'm struggling to think of ideas for my next book and I could do with some inspiration.'

'I'd love to come,' said Herbert.

'Aye, me an' all,' said Walter.

'I wouldn't miss it for the world, darling,' said Abigail. 'It's about time we had some fun.'

'We'll need some holiday reading,' said Herbert, taking a look through the shop's collection of second-hand books.

Walter joined him. Picking out a spooky book, he said, 'You like ghost stories, don't you, Herbert?'

'I do,' said Herbert.

'These are *true* stories,' said Walter, 'about *real* ghosts.' He read out the title: '*The Ghosts of Devon.*'

'Devon?' said Herbert, taking the book from Walter. '*We're* in Devon.' He looked warily at the illustration of the Wicked Lady on the cover, a ghost with shadowy eyes, who rode in a coach that was made of bones and decorated with skulls. 'I really hope we don't run into her,' he said with a shudder.

The next morning, after an early breakfast, Sunny's dad opened the back of the van and lifted in the item that was to be delivered to the Hotel Splendid. When Sunny came downstairs and saw what it was that they were delivering, he said, 'That's Mary and Elsie's rocking chair! They must have been missing it!'

He was eager to get going, as were the ghosts. They were all ready and waiting, apart from Abigail who was fretting over her reflection in the mirror on the door of her wardrobe. She was wearing the peasant dress that she had worn in her most recent crowd scene. What a shame, she thought, that she was not wearing a lovelier dress, and perhaps a fancy hat and some

costume jewellery. What a shame that she had been wearing this ragged old frock when, in the middle of a performance, she had fallen through a trap door in the stage. What a shame that she had been wearing this shabby number when all the other peasants fell through the trap door and landed on top of her. The last thing she remembered was feeling rather squashed. 'I do wish I was wearing something a little smarter,' she said, 'something suitable for the Hotel Splendid.'

'At least you've not got your pyjamas on,' said Herbert, who was always dressed for bedtime.

'Time to go!' called Sunny's dad, and, 'Holiday, here we come!' called Sunny's mum, as they came through the shop with the suitcases.

Sunny and the ghosts headed outside. Sunny helped the ghosts into the back of the van. It was only when Herbert and Walter and Abigail were in that Sunny realised Violet was missing. Looking around, he saw that she had gone back into the shop, which was now locked. She was at the door, visible through the glass, looking worried. Not all of the ghosts were able to go through walls and doors. Violet could not and was in danger of being left behind.

His dad, behind the wheel with his seatbelt on, called to Sunny, 'In you get, let's go!'

'But Dad,' said Sunny. 'Violet's still in the shop.'

His dad turned and looked at the shop, but Sunny

knew that he could not see Violet. Nonetheless, his dad said, 'Well, we can't leave Violet behind, can we?' He passed the keys to Sunny, who went to the door of the shop and unlocked it.

'I nearly left my notepad behind,' explained Violet as she hurried through the doorway and climbed into the back of the van.

Sunny locked up again and climbed into the front of the van. 'Thanks, Dad,' he said, handing back the keys.

'Thank you so much,' said Violet from the back.

'You're welcome,' said Sunny's dad, and they set off, heading for the seaside and the Hotel Splendid.

CHAPTER THREE

The Ghosts

ANA AND HER mum were in the hotel dining room eating their breakfast. Ana's mum picked up the teapot and said to Ana, 'Would you like some jam to go on your toast?'

'Yes please,' said Ana, who was concentrating on spreading her butter evenly.

Her mum finished filling her teacup and then said, 'I'll go and get you some.'

'Oh, no need,' said Ana, 'it's right here.' And there it was, right in front of her.

'So it is,' said her mum. 'I didn't see it there. Now . . .' She looked around the table. 'I could do with some milk for my tea.' Ana picked up the pot of jam and tried to get the lid off, but it was stiff so her mum reached over to help her. When the lid was off and Ana was spooning jam onto her toast, her mum said, 'All right, I'll just go and get some milk.'

'There's a jug of milk right there, Mum,' said Ana. And so there was, next to the teapot.

Ana's mum poured the milk into her teacup. 'It's funny,' she said, 'how something can be right in front of you and you just don't see it.'

As they left the dining room and crossed the foyer, they saw Mrs Griffin inspecting the post at the bottom of the stairs. 'I could have sworn this post was loose,' she said, 'but now it's just fine.'

'How long have you been here?' asked Mrs Sharma.

'Only a minute or so,' said Mrs Griffin, 'but that's long enough to tell if a post is wobbly.'

'I mean,' said Mrs Sharma, 'how long have you owned the hotel?'

'Oh,' said Mrs Griffin. 'Nearly a year now. The previous owners left suddenly, selling the place cheaply. I'd always wanted to run a seaside hotel. When I realised I could afford to buy the Hotel Splendid, I thought my dream had come true. The hotel was getting hardly any guests but I was determined to make a success of it. I thought I could breathe new life into the place. I've refurbished all the bedrooms, and I'm planning on having the foyer and the dining room redecorated, and I'm updating the website. It's a very old building though, and it has . . . some rather odd quirks.' She glanced at the bell on the reception desk. 'And—' Pausing, she seemed to change her mind about what she had been going to say. Instead, she said, 'Did you sleep well?'

'Eventually,' said Ana's mum, yawning. 'Did you have a late arrival?'

'A late arrival?' said Mrs Griffin.

'A guest arriving late, around midnight,' said Ana's mum.

'No,' said Mrs Griffin, looking concerned. 'I locked up at ten o'clock and went to bed.'

'I heard clattering and bumping at midnight,' said Ana's mum, 'like something being carried up the stairs and along the corridor. I thought it must be a guest with luggage. Maybe I was dreaming.'

But Ana had heard it too: the clattering and bumping, someone creeping about in the corridor, and, though it seemed a bit strange, she could have sworn that she had smelt paint.

In the middle of the morning, while Ana and her mum were up in their room getting ready to go to the beach, Sunny's dad was parking the van outside the Hotel Splendid. The three of them climbed out of the front and Sunny let the ghosts out of the back.

At the entrance to the hotel, Sunny held the door open until all the ghosts were inside. Abigail was the first to reach the reception desk, and rang the bell. When a woman wearing a glittery dress came through the door behind the desk, Sunny's dad said to her, 'I've got a delivery for Mrs Griffin.'

'Oh, that's me,' she said.

Sunny's mum was looking at the bell. 'That's a clever device you've got,' she said. 'It rang before I touched it. Does it have some sort of motion sensor?'

'There seems to be something wrong with the mechanism,' said Mrs Griffin. 'It keeps ringing all by itself.'

Sunny said to his mum, 'Abigail rang it,' but his mum just smiled at him.

'I wasn't expecting a delivery,' said Mrs Griffin.

'I've got it outside in the van,' said Sunny's dad, 'and I've got the paperwork here.' He showed Mrs Griffin the order.

She agreed that the order did seem to have come from the hotel; it was even on the proper hotel station-ery. 'But this isn't my handwriting,' she said. 'I can't think who would have sent this. I'm the only one here, apart from my guests.'

'You didn't order a rocking chair?' asked Sunny's dad.

'No,' said Mrs Griffin.

Sunny said, 'I expect Mary and Elsie ordered it. It's their rocking chair.'

'Who are Mary and Elsie?' asked Mrs Griffin.

'They're ghosts,' said Sunny.

'Ghosts?' said Mrs Griffin.

'Sunny . . .' said his mum.

Mrs Griffin turned back to Sunny's dad. 'May I see the rocking chair?'

'Of course,' said Sunny's dad, and he took her out to the van to show her the rocking chair.

When they came back in, Sunny's dad was carrying the rocking chair and Mrs Griffin was saying how well it would go with the decor. The rocking chair was placed in a corner of the foyer, and Sunny's mum said, 'It goes very well there.'

'Yes,' said Mrs Griffin. 'It looks like it belongs here, doesn't it?'

Having dealt with the delivery – which Mrs Griffin paid for with the last of the money in her till – Sunny's dad said that they were in fact going to be staying at the Hotel Splendid for the week. 'I phoned yesterday evening and booked a room.'

'Ah yes,' said Mrs Griffin, looking at her computer screen. 'I've put you in one of our two attic rooms. I'll show you the way.'

Herbert, Walter, Violet and Abigail decided to wait in the foyer – there was a comfy old velvet sofa on which they could sit and recover from the journey – while Sunny and his parents set off up the stairs with Mrs Griffin. At the same time, Ana and her mum were coming down, carrying a beach bag and a beach ball. When they met halfway up and halfway down the flight of stairs, Ana's mum stopped to say good morning to Mrs Griffin, and to Mrs Griffin's new guests.

Mrs Griffin said, 'Off to the beach?'

Sunny's mum said, 'Lovely weather!'

Sunny shouted, 'Mary!' and everyone looked at him in surprise. He was gazing with delight at the ghost he could see descending the stairs behind Ana and her mum. The ghost, finding that she could not get past the little knot of guests, braced herself and went through them, passing through Ana, who widened her eyes.

Ana stared at the figure that had just appeared in front of her. 'A ghost!' she said. 'I can see a ghost!'

Ana's mum looked at Mrs Griffin with embarrassment and began to explain: 'She likes to pretend. She's joined a drama club where they do things like drinking out of a cup that isn't really there. She can play throw and catch with a non-existent ball. She can put on invisible trousers. Ana, show Mrs Griffin your invisible trousers.'

'I really can see a ghost,' said Ana.

'It's all those ghost stories you read,' said her mum. 'They've got you imagining things. You read a scary ghost story, you think you see a scary ghost.'

'It's not scary,' said Ana, as Mary hugged Sunny and ruffled his curly hair. 'It looks very friendly.'

'Perhaps you're dehydrated,' said Mrs Sharma. 'It's a very warm day.' She rummaged in the beach bag. 'Dehydration can cause hallucinations.' She rummaged some more. 'I must have left the water bottle in our room,' she said. 'Wait here, I'll go and get it.' She headed back up the stairs, and Mrs Griffin set off again with Sunny's parents. Sunny asked if he could stay downstairs, and his mum and dad – seeing that he was standing with Ana, who was around his own age – said yes, he could stay and make friends, and that when they came back down they would all go out.

While the grown-ups headed up to the attic rooms, Mary led Sunny across the foyer, saying, 'Let's go and find Elsie.' Ana watched them, and saw another ghost, identical to the one that had just come down the stairs, coming out of the dining room.

'Elsie!' said Sunny. He ran towards the dining room, towards Elsie, who stopped in the doorway with a smile on her ghostly face. 'Hello, Elsie!' he said, trying to hug her ghostly figure, which was like trying to hug the air.

Elsie and Mary were also pleased to see Herbert and Walter and Violet, who had come hurrying over. The twins had never met Abigail, so Sunny introduced them.

When Mrs Griffin came downstairs again, having shown Sunny's parents to their room, she found Ana standing at the bottom of the stairs, looking around in amazement. Joining her, Mrs Griffin said, 'Did I hear you say you can see a ghost?'

'Yes,' said Ana.

'I don't believe in ghosts,' said Mrs Griffin. 'But—' She had the same look on her face as she'd had before, when she had mentioned the hotel's odd quirks and had seemed about to say something more but then changed her mind. This time, she went ahead and said it: 'I've been hearing strange noises ever since I moved in here.' She sighed. 'The hotel's occasional guests hear the noises too. They complain about being disturbed by somebody going up and down the stairs during the night, when there's no one else in the hotel. They hear sounds in the small hours - banging that they say sounds like hammering, and a raspy sound like sandpapering – sounds I can't explain. I could almost believe that there really is a ghost.'

'There's more than one,' said Ana.

Mrs Griffin shook her head. 'I expect there's some other explanation – noisy old plumbing, or seagulls scratching about on the window ledges and the roof.'

Sunny came over, bringing the ghosts to meet Mrs Griffin and Ana. Mrs Griffin watched Ana saying, 'Hello . . . Hello . . . It's lovely to meet you . . '. Hello . . .'

Mrs Griffin played along, pretending to shake invisible hands, saying, 'How do you do! How do you do!' while the ghosts stood a few feet away, watching this strange behaviour. When Mrs Griffin had shaken three or four invisible hands, she said to Ana, 'How many are there, dear?'

'There are six of them,' said Ana.

'Are there really? Goodness me!' said Mrs Griffin, in a tone that made Ana suspect that if she said to Mrs Griffin that she was off for a ride on her unicorn now, Mrs Griffin would say, in exactly the same tone, 'Are you really? Goodness me!'

'But usually,' said Sunny, 'there are only two.'

'I see,' said Mrs Griffin. 'How long have they been here?'

'Mary and Elsie have been here since the beginning

of May,' said Sunny. He counted the months on his fingers and added, 'They've been here for three months.'

'Well, please could you ask them to keep the noise down?' said Mrs Griffin with a laugh.

Mary and Elsie looked embarrassed. 'I'm so sorry,' said Mary.

Still chuckling, Mrs Griffin headed to the reception desk to deal with some paperwork.

Mary explained to Sunny, 'We try to keep away from the windows so that nobody sees us, but yesterday I couldn't resist looking out – our room has such a lovely view of the seafront. While I was standing at the window, a child suddenly turned and looked at me. I was so afraid of being seen that I backed away too quickly and knocked over a table and everything on it. It made a terrible noise. It damaged the table too. The leg wobbles now.'

'We don't mean to put people off coming here,' said Elsie. 'The hotel gets hardly any guests as it is. Those that do come leave bad reviews on TripAdvisor and don't come back. They say the place is weird. They complain about hearing strange noises and sleeping badly. I heard Mrs Griffin say that if the hotel doesn't start getting more guests soon, it will have to close.' Elsie and Mary looked very sad about this. 'We do try to keep quiet.'

Mary said to Elsie, 'You do keep ringing the bell though.'

'I do keep ringing the bell,' admitted Elsie. 'I get so excited when a guest comes into the foyer. I'm only trying to help. I love helping out on the reception desk and in the dining room at mealtimes, fetching all the little things that the guests need.'

'The funny thing is,' said Mary, 'we hear strange noises too, after Mrs Griffin has gone to bed, even if there are no guests.'

'Mrs Griffin thinks it's the plumbing, or seagulls,' said Ana.

'Yes,' said Mary, 'that must be it.'

Mrs Sharma was coming down the stairs with a bottle of water which she handed to Ana. 'Here,' she said, 'drink this.' Ana drank some of the water and then her mum said, 'Now, have the ghosts gone?'

'No,' said Ana, 'they're still here.'

'Hmm,' said Mrs Sharma, frowning at Ana. 'Aha! I see the problem. You haven't got your glasses on. That's no doubt given you a headache, causing you to see things that aren't there. You wait here while I go back up to our room to fetch your glasses.'

Mrs Sharma left again and Ana looked around at the ghosts. 'You are there, aren't you?' she said.

'Oh yes, dear,' said Elsie, and there was general agreement from all the ghosts that they really were there.

'I've always wanted to see a ghost,' said Ana. 'I've been to lots and lots of places that are supposed to be haunted, but I've never actually seen a ghost until now.'

Sunny looked at her and said with a smile, 'You've just given me an idea.'

Violet turned to a new page in her notepad, ready to write down Sunny's idea. Sunny said, 'I think—'

'What are you writing, Violet?' asked Herbert.

'I'm working on a new story,' said Violet.

'How exciting!' said Herbert. 'What's it about?'

'It's about Sunny and all of us,' said Violet. She flipped back through the pages and showed Herbert the title that she had written down: *Sunny and the Hotel Splendid*. 'I've written about Mary and Elsie's postcard arriving, and about driving here in the van and delivering their rocking chair. Now I'm writing about this.'

Herbert looked at the page on which Violet had been writing, at the top of which it said, *Violet turned to a new page in her notepad, ready to write down Sunny's idea.*

'Or at least I'm *trying* to,' said Violet. She interrupted Sunny to say, 'Would you mind starting again? I missed all that. Herbert was talking to me and I got distracted.'

'Sorry, Violet,' said Herbert.

'*Sorry, Violet,' said Herbert*, wrote Violet. 'That's all right, Herbert,' said Violet.

When Violet was ready, Sunny said, 'I think we need to let people know you're here.'

'Let people know I'*m* here?' asked Violet, whose first book had recently been published and who was hoping that some people had read it and liked it. 'Oh! Do you think people will want my autograph?' She was enjoying being a writer. She even had her own website. Sunny had helped her to make it, using a computer in the shop. 'Will they want to take my photograph?'

'I mean all of you,' said Sunny. 'We need to let people know there are ghosts here.'

'But we've been trying very hard *not* to let people know we're here,' said Elsie. 'I know they've heard us, and they complain.'

'I think that's the problem,' said Sunny. 'They hear strange noises and sleep badly and that's what they complain about. They're not complaining about you, because they don't know about you.'

'If people knew that the noises were caused by

33

ghosts,' said Ana, 'they might want to come here. Lots of people love going to places that are said to be haunted, and they're disappointed when they don't see anything spooky.'

'But people *can't* see us,' said Elsie. 'At least the grown-ups can't.'

'That's true,' agreed Ana, 'but we can still show them you're here.' She held out the beach ball. 'If you throw this to Herbert . . .' Elsie took the beach ball from Ana and threw it to Herbert, who caught it.

'Good catch, Herbert,' said Sunny.

'Thank you,' said Herbert proudly. 'I've been practising.' He threw the ball back to Elsie. It arced between them.

'If they saw that, for example,' said Ana, 'they might have to believe in you.' She looked at Mary rocking gently in the rocking chair, and at Violet scribbling in her notepad, and at Abigail in her old-fashioned costume. 'Would anyone be interested,' said Ana, 'in putting on a play?'

CHAPTER FOUR

The Play

'YOU'LL ALL HAVE a role,' said Ana. 'Elsie, you can ring the bell on the reception desk.'

'Oh yes,' said Elsie, looking pleased, 'I can do that.'

To Mary, rocking in the rocking chair, Ana said, 'That's great, Mary. Could you keep doing that?'

'That suits me very well,' said Mary.

'Violet,' said Ana, 'have you ever written a script?'

'I haven't,' said Violet, 'but I'd love to have a go.'

'I wish we could have someone playing this piano,' said Ana, 'but Mrs Griffin said it doesn't work.'

'That's not a piano,' said Walter. 'That's a pump organ. I haven't seen one in years. There's a knack to playing a pump organ. Let's have a look.' He walked over to it, pulled out some of the knobs and pumped the pedals with his feet. When he pressed down on the keys, they all heard the sound of the organ.

Mrs Griffin came into the foyer with a look of

delight on her face. Seeing Ana standing near the pump organ, she said to her, 'You've got it working! How wonderful. It's a pity I don't have any sheet music.'

'That's all right,' said Walter. 'I can play without sheet music.'

'Mrs Griffin,' said Ana, 'is it all right if we put on a play in the foyer?'

'That sounds like fun,' said Mrs Griffin, and she promised to come and watch.

At that moment, Mrs Sharma came down the stairs with Ana's glasses and made her put them on. 'That should get rid of the ghosts,' she said. Ana turned and looked through her glasses at Violet.

'Nope,' said Violet, 'we're still here!'

'I'm exhausted after going up and down all those stairs,' said Mrs Sharma. 'I need a rest.' She sat down in the rocking chair. 'This is a very nice chair,' she said, 'but it's not as comfortable as it looks.'

'This *is* rather uncomfortable,' agreed Mary.

'Come with me, Mrs Sharma,' said Mrs Griffin. 'I'll find you somewhere more comfortable to sit. Would you like a cup of tea?' Mrs Sharma said that would be lovely. She told Ana that she could play with her new friend until lunchtime, and followed Mrs Griffin out of the foyer.

'Herbert,' said Ana, 'you'll be in charge of lighting.'

Herbert saluted.

'All right,' said Ana. 'So you all know what you're doing: Violet's writing the script, Walter's playing the pump organ, Herbert's in charge of the lights, Elsie's ringing the bell, and Mary's in the rocking chair.'

Abigail, who had been waiting expectantly to hear her own name, wilted with disappointment.

'And Abigail,' said Ana, walking over to her. 'You're going to be the ghost that haunts the Hotel Splendid.'

'Oh!' said Abigail. 'Yes! I'm sure I could give a very convincing performance as a spooky ghost.'

Violet turned to a clean page in her notepad and wondered how to begin. Some of the second-hand books in the shop were plays, some of which she had read. They always started by saying where the scene was taking place: *Macbeth* began in a desert place during a thunderstorm, and *Hamlet* began on the ramparts of a royal castle. Neatly, at the top of the page, she wrote: 'The foyer of the Hotel Splendid'. She wrote directions for all the ghosts, so that they would know what to do when, and she wrote a few lines of dialogue for Abigail. Now and again, she consulted the others: 'How will Abigail know when she's supposed to enter?' she asked, and, 'What are you going to play on the pump organ, Walter?'

Walter thought about all the tunes he played on the piano in the shop, and which one he would like to try playing on the pump organ. 'I think,' he said, 'I would like to play the tune our Herbert has been composing.'

'Oh Walter,' said Herbert. His ghostly eyes seemed to well up with ghostly tears. 'My composition performed in a play. Well I never.'

'That's an excellent choice,' said Violet. 'It's such an eerie piece of music.'

'Thank you,' said Herbert. 'I used all the keys, the black ones and the white ones, and some of them more than once.'

When the script was finished, Violet made copies and handed them out, then everyone got into position ready for the rehearsal. Elsie, behind the reception desk, gave the bell a few dozen trial dings, and Herbert found the dimmer switch and started twiddling it to and fro. 'All right,' said Mary, 'that's enough, you'll give me a headache.'

Ana and Abigail went up the stairs until they were just out of sight. 'I haven't even brushed my hair,' said Abigail, touching her ghostly hair with her ghostly hand.

'You look perfect for the part,' said Ana, and Abigail beamed.

Abigail studied her first line of dialogue and cleared her throat. 'Ohhh . . .' she said. 'Like that? Or more like this?' She took a deep breath. 'Ooohhh!'

She tried out different types of wailing until Ana said, 'Yes, that's it, do that one.'

The foyer of the Hotel Splendid

MARY is sitting in a rocking chair, rocking to and fro.

GUESTS enter through the front door.

ELSIE rings the bell on the reception desk.

ABIGAIL descends the staircase, wailing.

    ABIGAIL: Oh, woe is me.

WALTER begins playing eerie music on the pump organ.

HERBERT fiddles with the dimmer switch, making the
  lights flicker.

ABIGAIL crosses the foyer.

    ABIGAIL: Oh, I am doomed to haunt the rooms and
               corridors of the Hotel Splendid for evermore...

Abigail learnt her lines, with Ana's help. 'Oh, woe is me,' said Abigail. 'Oh, I am doomed to haunt the rooms and corridors of the Hotel Splendour for evermore.'

'Splendid,' said Ana.

'Thank you,' said Abigail.

'No,' said Ana, 'I mean, you said the Hotel Splendour but it's the Hotel Splendid.'

'Oh yes,' said Abigail. 'I'll try that again.'

While the ghosts were rehearsing, Sunny was working hard designing flyers, using paper and felt-tip pens that Elsie found behind the reception desk. When Ana saw his design, she said it was brilliant and that lots of people were sure to come along and see their play.

Experience the
HAUNTED
Hotel Splendid

Today at 3pm

At lunchtime, Sunny and Ana went out with their parents. The two families decided to go together to a nearby cafe. Sunny took the flyers with him, and gave one to the cafe owner, who agreed to display it in the front window. The rest of the flyers they handed out on the promenade and on the beach.

The ghosts had decided to stay behind at the hotel. Walter was keen to practise Herbert's tune on the pump organ, and Abigail said she needed to go over her lines. Herbert and Mary wanted to rest, and Elsie – thinking that it would be nice to offer their visitors afternoon tea – was busy in the kitchen.

In the middle of the afternoon, the ghosts were still rehearsing and resting and waiting when Sunny and Ana opened the door, peeked into the foyer and said, 'Are you ready?'

Violet glimpsed a small crowd of people who had gathered outside: as well as Sunny and Ana's parents, there were about a dozen other people, a mixture of grown-ups and children. She heard someone saying, 'Is this the haunted hotel?'

With butterflies in her ghostly stomach, Violet clapped her hands and said, 'Positions, everyone!' Abigail dashed up the stairs, Walter flexed his hands at the pump organ, and Mary rocked back and forth in her chair.

Outside, Ana took a deep breath and said to the

group, 'Welcome to the Hotel Splendid. If you would care to follow me inside, you might be lucky enough to see the ghost that is doomed to haunt the rooms and corridors of the Hotel Splendid for evermore.'

As soon as everyone was inside, Elsie rang the bell on the reception desk. The grown-ups looked towards the bell that appeared to have rung all on its own, and the children gasped.

The sound of the bell brought Mrs Griffin into the foyer. She was astonished to see so many people there. From upstairs came the sound of a scream, surprising everyone who heard it. The children turned their heads towards the staircase, down which came Abigail. Her ghostly hair was tangled and her ghostly dress was ragged and she cried out, 'Oh, woe is me!'

Walter, hearing his cue, played the opening bars of Herbert's eerie music.

A man, staring at the organ, seeing the keys and the pedals moving, said, 'I've always wanted to see one that plays by itself.'

Herbert, standing by the dimmer switch, made the lights in the foyer flicker from bright to dim to bright again. The grown-ups looked up at the lights and a child said, 'It's a ghost! A ghost is doing it!'

Abigail crossed the foyer, pausing in front of the group to say, 'Oh! Oh! I am doomed to haunt the rooms and corridors of the Hotel Splendid for

evermore . . .' She hurried on across the foyer and disappeared through the wall. A boy ran after her and touched the wall just where she had gone through. 'She went through the wall!' he said. 'It's a solid wall but she walked straight through it!'

The grown-ups looked questioningly at Mrs Griffin, who said uncertainly, 'Welcome to the Hotel Splendid.'

'Which is haunted,' said Ana.

'It's not haunted,' said Mrs Griffin, laughing nervously.

One family left quickly, looking worried, and Mrs Griffin said to Sunny and Ana, 'You're scaring people away!' But the boy who had run after Abigail returned to his dad saying, 'Let's go and tell Mum. She'll have to come and see for herself.' Meanwhile, other people were snapping pictures and typing messages on their phones.

'Would anybody care for afternoon tea?' asked Elsie, who had put teacups and a pot of tea and glasses and a jug of squash and plates of cake and biscuits out on a table.

'How on earth have you managed all this?' said Mrs Griffin to Sunny and Ana, who were pouring the drinks and handing round the cake and biscuits.

'Elsie did it,' said Ana.

Mrs Griffin looked at Ana's mum, who said, 'Perhaps your blood sugar is a little low, Ana. You should have something to eat,' and she passed her a flapjack.

The guests said to one another what a refreshing cup of tea, what delicious cake, and returned to the promenade still talking loudly about what they had just experienced.

When the group had left, Abigail put her head back through the wall and said, 'How was that?'

The other ghosts clapped and cheered, and Violet congratulated Abigail on her improvisation. 'What a good idea to end the scene by disappearing through the wall,' she said. 'You should do that every time. I'll add that to the script.'

Herbert asked, 'Did I do all right?'

'Your work with the dimmer switch was wonderful,' said Violet. 'The lighting was just as I'd imagined.'

The grown-ups wanted to know how the children had done it – the eerie music, the flickering lights, and all the rest of it.

'It wasn't us,' said Sunny, 'it was the ghosts. They were fantastic.'

'Thank you, darling,' said Abigail, who was resting on the velvet sofa with her ghostly feet in Elsie's ghostly lap.

'Thank you, dear,' said Mary, who was still rocking in the rocking chair. Ana's mum watched the chair rocking to and fro and asked if the chair had a motor.

'I have a reclining chair with a motor,' she said to Sunny's mum, 'and I once had a go in a chair that vibrated.'

'It's not a motor,' said Ana, 'it's a ghost.'

'It might just be a draught,' said Sunny's mum. 'When it did that in the shop, it was caused by a draught.'

'It's a ghost,' said Ana.

Ana's mum said to Sunny's mum, 'Yes, perhaps that's what it is, a draught.'

They were still discussing the performance when a woman came into the hotel, introducing herself as a reporter for the local newspaper. With her was a young man wearing a suit and carrying a camera – he looked like a recent school leaver on his first job. Greeted by Mrs Griffin, the reporter asked her about the ghost: 'People are saying that the Hotel Splendid is haunted.'

Mrs Griffin laughed and said, 'You won't find any ghosts here!'

'Positions, everyone!' called Violet.

Elsie got up and made her way over to the reception desk to ring the bell, though she was obviously tired. In fact, all the ghosts were tired from the first performance. Their second performance was full of mistakes. First, Abigail fluffed her cue because she was still downstairs and so could not *come* downstairs when the bell rang. Elsie had to ring the bell three times before Abigail finally launched into her first line. Then Walter kept pressing the wrong keys on the pump organ. Herbert twisted the dimmer switch too far and everything went dark. There was a shriek and a swear word. Herbert said, 'Sorry!' and brought the lights up again. Abigail, distracted by these mistakes, forgot her lines. 'Oh!' she said, pausing in front of the young man with the camera. He seemed almost to be able to see her and hear her, as if he caught a glimpse of her out of the corner of his eye but lost her when he tried to look right at her; as if he heard her voice as a whisper but could not quite make out the words. 'Oh!' said Abigail. She glanced at Violet.

'I am doomed . . .' whispered Violet.

'Oh yes! I am doomed!' said Abigail. 'To haunt the rooms and corridors of the Hotel Splendour for evermore . . .'

'Splendid,' whispered Violet.

'Thank you,' whispered Abigail.

But none of these errors really spoiled the performance. If anything, the repeated ringing of the bell and the off-key music and the plunge into darkness made the atmosphere in the hotel foyer even spookier.

The reporter was looking around the foyer, her eyes wide, her mouth hanging open.

Mrs Griffin said, 'It's just . . .' She looked over at the bell on the reception desk, and up at the light.

'. . . the plumbing . . . or seagulls . . .'

'The Hotel Splendid really is haunted,' said Sunny. The reporter wrote that down in her notepad.

'And it does afternoon tea,' said Elsie.

'And it does the best afternoon tea in Devon,' said Sunny. Elsie beamed.

The reporter beckoned the young man with the camera. 'May we take some photographs?' she asked.

Abigail came back through the wall to meet the reporter and the photographer. 'Of course you may, darling,' she said. 'Where do you want me – on the staircase where I make my grand entrance? How exciting – my first photo shoot!'

On Monday morning, a story about the haunted hotel's mournful ghost appeared on the front page of a local newspaper. The following morning, it was mentioned in all the other local papers, and at the same time word was getting around on social media. People phoned to ask if the story was true, and to book a room.

Mrs Griffin did not book out room one. She still had not found the key. This was just as well because it was the room in which Mary and Elsie were staying,

and which they were now sharing with their friends. There was a place for everyone:

Mary and Elsie liked to rest on the twin beds.

Abigail liked to sit on the windowsill, looking out at all the people going by. It would take some time for Mary and Elsie to get used to the idea that they did not have to stay away from the windows, but they liked to hear Abigail talking about what she could see.

There was space on the windowsill for Walter when he felt like company, and there was a wardrobe for when he needed a rest.

There was a table at which Violet could sit and work. It was the same table that Mary had knocked over, and Violet tested it for the wobble that Mary said it now had, but it seemed perfectly all right, and when she said so, Mary came over to have a look and had to agree that it really was fine now, somehow. Violet opened her notepad and settled down to write. She had discovered that she liked scriptwriting, and was working on a new play.

Herbert liked the armchair, which had two cushions and was very comfortable. He sat there reading and listening out for noises.

In the middle of the week, in the small hours, a guest left his room and crept along the corridor and up the stairs, looking for the ghost that he had heard about. Meanwhile, another guest in another room

heard floorboards creaking in the corridor, and foot-
steps on the stairs.

At dawn, Sunny, still in his pyjamas, sneaked
down to room one. When he knocked, Elsie opened
the door. Herbert was sitting in the armchair, reading
The Ghosts of Devon and looking nervous. Glancing
up suddenly, Herbert said, 'What's that noise?'

'It's just me, Herbert,' said Sunny, coming in.

'No,' said Herbert, 'another noise, downstairs . . .
Listen . . .'

'I can't hear anything,' said Violet. 'It's just your
imagination.' She said to Sunny, 'He's been up all
night reading these ghost stories and they've made
him jumpy.'

'Wait,' said Sunny. He listened, and heard a faint
clattering noise. 'I can hear something. It must be Mrs
Griffin.'

'But she's never up at this time,' said Elsie.

Now Sunny could hear a rumbling noise. He said,
'It sounds like something being rolled or wheeled
through the foyer.'

'Yes,' said Herbert, 'and that's exactly what the
Wicked Lady's coach of bones would sound like!'

'It won't be her,' said Sunny. 'How would she get
her coach inside the building?'

'It's a *ghost* coach,' said Herbert. 'Ghostly posses-
sions can take on ghostly properties. She could easily

ride her coach into the hotel and across the foyer. She could probably ride it up the stairs if she wanted.'

Just at that moment, they heard, very clearly, a noise on the stairs. Herbert stifled a shriek.

'It won't be her,' insisted Sunny, though he didn't sound so sure now. Cautiously, he peeped outside, looking up and down the corridor. 'There's no one there,' he said.

'You've got us all imagining things now, Herbert,' said Violet.

'No,' said Herbert. 'I did hear something, and you all heard it too.' And everyone, including Violet, had to admit that was true.

In the morning, over breakfast, one guest said to another, 'I heard the ghost outside my door last night. I convinced myself to get out of bed and go and look. I *know* I heard something, but when I opened the door, there was nothing there.'

Meanwhile, the man who had gone looking for a ghost during the night was saying to another guest that he had certainly heard *something*.

The few children in the dining room could see Elsie

going from table to table, looking to see if anyone needed anything. The children pointed her out to their parents, who looked and said, 'There's nothing there,' although they never sounded entirely sure.

'I have a couple of friends,' said the man, 'who are keen ghosthunters. If there is a ghost in this hotel, I bet my friends can find it and catch it. I made a phone call this morning. They're going to pay the hotel a visit.'

'Oh my,' said Elsie, who did not like the sound of this. She hurried out of the dining room. She had to warn the ghosts that the ghosthunters were coming.

CHAPTER FIVE

The Ghosthunters

T HE STORY ABOUT the haunted hotel had been picked up by the national newspapers, and Mrs Griffin's telephone had been ringing non-stop. Elsie tried to help by answering some of the calls, but the person on the other end could never hear her. This only added to the hotel's reputation though, and new guests continued to arrive.

At least once a day, the ghosts gave a performance. Sunny worried that they would exhaust themselves, but Abigail said that she was thoroughly enjoying herself, and Walter said that he had not had this much fun in years. Elsie was delighted that the hotel was so busy, and Mary said that she only had to sit and rock and that was fine by her.

By the end of the week, all of Mrs Griffin's rooms had been booked out to guests, with the exception of the room on the first floor that was being used by the

ghosts. The last of her guests, who she put in a room at the end of the third floor, were Shaun and Sheena Shackleton, who arrived with what Mrs Griffin called a surprising amount of interesting equipment.

'It's for finding your ghost,' said Shaun.

'Oh,' said Mrs Griffin. 'I doubt you'll find one.'

'If there's a ghost here,' said Shaun, 'we'll find it. How could we not find it with all this equipment? We've got everything we need.' He showed her his camcorder, which had night vision so that he could film the ghosthunt and put it on YouTube. He showed her a motion sensor, a temperature sensor and an energy sensor, for detecting movement and sudden changes in temperature and energy.

'Oh my,' said Elsie, hurrying up the stairs to tell the others.

When Elsie had explained to the ghosts that the ghosthunters were downstairs and that they had an awful lot of equipment with them, Mary, Abigail and Herbert started looking for somewhere to hide. They decided on Walter's wardrobe, into which they piled, startling Walter who was already in there. Meanwhile, Violet crept out of the room and down the stairs, spying on the ghosthunters through the banisters, wanting to get a good look at them so that she could describe them in her story.

They were both wearing camouflage: camouflage

T-shirts, camouflage cargo shorts and camouflage caps. In addition to the handheld devices that they kept in their utility belts and which Shaun had been demonstrating to Mrs Griffin, there was a larger item of equipment on wheels, a container with a suction tube attached, looking all in all much like Mrs Griffin's vacuum cleaner except that it was made of metal and did not have her vacuum cleaner's friendly face. 'And when we find your ghost,' said Shaun, 'this is for catching it.'

On the ghosthunters' first night at the hotel, in the hour before dawn, Violet heard sounds coming from the corridor above and on the stairs. She was longing to have a look and see if it was them, but she could not go through doors. Slowly, carefully, she turned the door handle and eased the door open just a crack. She peeked out. There, at the bottom of the stairs, was Sheena, studying the energy sensor; and there was Shaun, eating a cheese and pickle sandwich. Brushing crumbs off the front of his T-shirt, he said to Sheena, 'Are you getting a reading here?'

'Not yet,' said Sheena.

'Can you see the ghosthunters?' whispered Herbert, right into Violet's ear, making her jump.

'Not well enough,' said Violet. She was keen to see the energy sensor close up. 'I'm going to get a better look.'

'I think it would be wise to stay out of their way,' said Herbert, sounding worried, but Violet was already out in the corridor. Herbert did not want her to be out there alone, so he went after her. When the door clicked shut behind Herbert, Sheena turned around. She looked hard at the closed door and then moved down the corridor, approaching room one.

The energy sensor looked a little bit like a remote control for a television, but with a row of lights along the top, ranging in colour from green to yellow to orange to red. The green and yellow lights were on and Sheena said, 'I'm picking something up.'

Violet said to Herbert, 'She's picking something up!' The reading was weak but definitely there.

'What if it's her?' said Herbert, looking petrified. 'What if it's the Wicked Lady?'

'Herbert,' said Violet, 'it's not the Wicked Lady.'

Shaun reached into one of the pouches on his utility belt, and Violet looked to see what contraption he would bring out, but it was another cheese and pickle sandwich. Shaun followed Sheena down the corridor, sandwich in one hand, ghost vacuum in the other.

Herbert gazed longingly at the sandwich, murmuring, 'I really miss cheese and pickle.'

Outside room one, Sheena came to a stop and studied the energy sensor. As well as the green and yellow lights, the orange light now blinked on. 'Yes,' she said. 'There's definitely something here.'

'I don't like this,' whispered Herbert.

The red light came on. Now the whole row was lit up.

'It's here!' said Sheena.

Herbert shrieked. 'It's here! It's here!' He turned and ran off towards the stairs.

'Herbert!' shouted Violet. 'It's not the Wicked Lady!'

'Is everything all right?' asked Walter, putting his head through the door. 'We can hear shouting and shrieking.'

'Herbert's scared of the ghosthunters,' said Violet, 'and the Wicked Lady.'

'Is she here?' asked Walter, looking worried.

From inside the room, Mary said to Walter, 'Who's here? What's happening?' and Walter pulled his head back into the room to say that Herbert was scared of the ghosthunters and the Wicked Lady.

Walter, re-emerging, coming fully into the corridor, said, 'I'd better go and see if Herbert's all right,' and he hurried down the stairs.

Violet could hear Mary through the door, saying, 'Walter says she *is* here . . . It *was* her . . .' Violet wanted to explain to Mary that the Wicked Lady was – probably – not in the hotel and that it was just a misunderstanding, but Mary, Elsie and Abigail were all talking excitedly and could not hear Violet through the door. Violet could not open the door without risking detection, because Sheena was standing very close to her, pointing the energy sensor in the direction of room one.

'I'm getting a very strong signal just here,' said Sheena, stepping forward into Violet, who yelped and darted away.

Violet fled down the stairs and into the dimly lit foyer, where she called out breathlessly, 'Walter? Herbert?' She heard a noise behind her, turned and saw a strange two-headed creature lurking behind the big potted palm tree. Violet muffled a scream. The creature waved its arms: one in a shirt sleeve and one in a pyjama sleeve. She looked at its feet: one in a boot and one in a slipper.

'Violet,' whispered one of the heads. 'Over here.'

'Is that you, Walter?' said Violet.

'Yes,' said the head.

'And me,' said the other head. 'We're hiding.'

Hearing footsteps at the top of the stairs, and coming down towards the foyer, Violet hurried over

and tried to hide herself behind the potted palm tree with Walter and Herbert, but it was no good, there was not enough space. The three of them darted over to the little reception desk and ducked down. They held their ghostly breath and listened, hearing foot-steps coming down the stairs, into the foyer, pausing in front of the reception desk.

'Is it her?' whimpered Herbert. 'Is it the Wicked Lady?'

'It won't be her,' said Walter, but he didn't sound very sure.

'Herbert,' said Violet, 'it's *us*. The ghosthunters' equipment was detecting *us*. *We* are the ghosts.'

From the far side of the desk came a ghostly, female voice, saying, 'Herbert? Herbert?'

Herbert trembled.

'Walter?' said the voice. 'Violet? Are you down here?'

'It's Abigail!' said Violet, peering over the desk. 'Abigail! Are you all right? Where are Mary and Elsie?'

'The ghosthunters have got them . . .' said Abigail.

'Oh no!' wailed Violet, thinking of that awful ghost vacuum, thinking of it hoovering up poor Mary, poor Elsie, who would be so terribly cramped in there, or who might now have ceased to exist at all; poor Mary and Elsie, who had loved the Hotel Splendid, who had loved being here by the sea . . .

'Violet,' said Abigail. 'Calm down. Listen. The ghosthunters have got them trapped in their room. I was able to escape but Mary and Elsie need our help. We have to distract the ghosthunters so that they'll come after us instead. I tried to get them to notice me – I did my lines, I wafted to and fro – but my ghostly aura alone isn't strong enough to take their attention away from Mary and Elsie. But if we all go, all four of us, I think we can do it.'

Violet, Walter and Herbert came out from behind the reception desk and hurried back upstairs with Abigail. Reaching room one, Abigail went through the door and opened it from the inside, letting in the others. Mary and Elsie were clinging to one another in the far corner of the room. Sheena, holding out the energy sensor, was advancing towards them. Not far behind her was Shaun, holding out the suction tube of the ghost vacuum with one hand while the index finger of his other hand reached for the ON switch. As the ghost vacuum roared to life, Shaun and Sheena turned to look at the suddenly wide-open door.

'Now,' said Abigail, 'what I propose doing is . . .'

'Leave them alone!' yelled Violet, taking a cushion from the armchair in which Herbert liked to sit, and throwing it at Sheena, who dropped the energy sensor in surprise. Violet reached for the other cushion and threw it at Shaun, whose arm was knocked sideways by the cushion, and whose suction tube sucked up a corner of the curtain instead. The noise it made was like somebody blowing a raspberry.

'Run!' yelled Violet, taking hold of Mary and Elsie and running with them to the door, which Walter was holding open for them.

'Come on, Herbert,' said Abigail, seeing him dilly-dallying dangerously close to the ghosthunters. 'We have to get out of here!' The two of them fled together, followed by Walter, who slammed the door behind him.

Down the stairs they ran, hearing the door of room one opening behind them. Abigail, in her panic, knocked a picture off the wall, and Sheena shouted out, 'Downstairs!'

Half the ghosts ran to the potted palm tree and tried to hide behind it.

'That's not big enough!' said Violet. 'I can see you!' She squatted down behind the reception desk, and the rest of the ghosts hurried over to join her. 'It's not big enough for all of us!' said Violet. The six of them spilled out again and ran wildly about the foyer, until Walter tried the door of the cupboard under the stairs and found that it opened, and he and Herbert and Mary and Elsie and Abigail and Violet all squeezed into that dark and just-big-enough space and closed the door.

They heard the ghosthunters coming down the stairs. They heard Sheena saying, 'It's down here somewhere.' They heard her voice moving towards the potted palm tree and the reception desk.

'She's going away,' said Walter.

'But she'll find us,' said Elsie, 'with her energy sensor. We're done for. There's no hiding from . . .' Her voice trailed off. She was looking at a row of lights: green, yellow, orange and red glowing brightly in the dark. 'What's that?' she said.

'It's the energy sensor,' said Herbert. 'She dropped it. I picked it up. I think I'd better put it somewhere safe.' He reached up and put it on a high shelf.

The ghosts were chuckling and starting to relax when the door was pulled open and there was Shaun, lifting the night-vision camcorder up to his eye. Through the lens, he was looking right at the ghosts.

'Please don't hurt us,' said Elsie.

The ghosts huddled together, looking fearfully at Shaun, and at the ghost vacuum in his hand.

'Please don't hoover us up,' said Mary.

Shaun sighed and called to Sheena, 'It's not in here.' He lowered the camcorder. 'We must have dozens of these videos on YouTube now, and there's not a ghost in any of them.'

Sheena made an exasperated sort of noise. 'We were so close to catching it!' she said. 'As usual.'

'One little ghost in this vast building, it could be anywhere,' said Shaun, closing the door on seven ghostly faces. It was almost dawn. 'Let's call it a night,' he said, and he and Sheena climbed the stairs, returning to their room to sleep through the day, taking their ghost vacuum with them.

After a moment, Herbert said, 'I'm glad they've gone.'

'Aye, me an' all,' said Walter.

'I'm *very* glad,' said Violet.

'So are we,' said Mary.

'Oh yes,' said Elsie.

'And good riddance,' said Abigail.

'That was close,' said a seventh voice.

Herbert nearly jumped out of his skin. All the ghosts turned to see who had spoken, but the cupboard was too dark.

'Is this better?' said the voice. A lightbulb came on overhead, and the ghost of a man in a tropical shirt said, 'Hello, I'm Alan.'

When the ghosts had got over their shock, Walter said, 'Sorry, Alan, is this *your* cupboard?' He looked around admiringly and added, 'It's a lovely one.'

'It is, isn't it?' said Alan, looking pleased. 'I fitted these shelves myself. They're very useful.'

'How long have you been here?' asked Elsie.

'Oh, I've been here for decades,' said Alan. 'I used to

own the hotel, but I'm afraid I ran it into the ground because I don't have a head for business. I do love the place though, and I'm good with my hands.' He held up his ghostly hands. 'I keep an eye on the place and do what I can to maintain it. I see to things that are wobbly and need fixing, and things that are shabby and need sanding and varnishing or painting. I water the potted palm tree. That's the sort of thing I'm good at. The exterior of the hotel could really do with some attention: the facade needs painting and some of the letters spelling out the name of the hotel need replacing.' He showed them the T, the L and the I that he had stored carefully in a corner of his neat and tidy cupboard. 'But,' he added, 'I don't have a ladder long enough to do it.'

'You've been here all this time, and we had no idea,' said Elsie.

'I prefer to stay out of the way in the daytime,' said Alan. 'I do most of my work at night.'

The ghosts could understand this.

'It's not ideal,' said Alan. 'It's hard to hammer silently. Tonight I've been doing what I thought would be a quiet job, filling cracks in the walls, but while I was fetching what I needed from my cupboard I knocked something over, and then I had to wheel the organ out of the way, and then wheel it back again, and it was all much noisier than I expected. But I seem to

67

be even more of a problem when I don't at least try to keep a low profile. I tried to make contact with the previous owners – I left little notes stuck to the computer screen, introducing myself: *Hello! I'm Alan from the cupboard under the stairs.* That sort of thing. They left quite suddenly, just like the ones before them. They didn't mention me when they sold the place to Mrs Griffin, and I haven't tried to make contact with her. I like her a lot and would hate her to leave.'

'My sister and I have been here since May,' said Elsie.

'Yes,' said Alan. 'I saw you arrive.'

'Why didn't you ever come and say hello to us?' asked Mary.

'I've spent so long with no one to talk to,' said Alan, 'or at least no one that could see me or hear me. I have been lonely but I've got used to keeping myself to myself. Also, you're *ghosts*. You're the first ghosts I've ever seen. You can't imagine how scared I was when I first realised there was a *ghost* in the hotel.'

'I can,' said Herbert sympathetically.

'And all of a sudden there were *lots* of ghosts.' He eyed the six ghostly faces now surrounding him. 'And I heard terrible wailing and the strangest organ music.'

'Didn't you like the music?' asked Herbert with concern.

'It gave me the creeps,' said Alan.

'Oh yes,' said Violet, 'it would do. It's a very powerful piece of work.'

'Anyway,' said Elsie, 'it's very nice to meet you now. And I think we might be able to help you.'

Over breakfast, Alan was introduced to Sunny and Ana, who were very excited to meet him. Alan apologised to Ana for keeping her and her mum awake on their first night at the hotel, with the noise he had made painting over the stain on the ceiling. 'I thought it would be a quiet job that wouldn't disturb you,' he said. 'But the stepladder was very clattery.'

'That's quite all right,' said Ana. 'It looks much better now.'

After breakfast, it was time to go home. When the two families brought their luggage down to reception, Mrs Griffin said to Sunny and Ana, 'I'm fully booked to the end of the year now. I won't have to close the hotel after all, thanks to you two.'

'It was mostly the ghosts,' said Sunny.

'Of course,' said Mrs Griffin. 'Thank you, ghosts!' She smiled at the air.

Violet, who was sitting on the velvet sofa, said, 'You're very welcome.'

Abigail, who'd been chatting with Mary and Elsie, said, 'A pleasure, darling.'

'And I've just about finished my story,' said Violet. 'I've only got the ending left to write.'

'Am I in your story?' asked Ana.

'Yes,' said Violet. 'In fact, I think I'll put you right at the start. Come and sit with me and tell me all about the day you arrived at the hotel.'

Ana sat down next to Violet and described the day of her arrival. 'We got here the day before you did,' she said. 'It was nearly teatime . . .'

Meanwhile, Mary was having a word with Sunny. 'Elsie and I have been talking to Abigail,' she said. 'The three of us have become good friends and Abigail is very happy here, aren't you, dear?'

'Oh yes, darling,' said Abigail. 'I'm very happy.'

'We've invited her to stay here, with us,' said Mary. 'Also, she's such an important part of the performance – she's the star. Elsie and I can manage everything else. Walter's shown me how to play a tune on the pump organ, and Elsie's going to ring the bell and rock the chair and do the lights.'

'Can you manage all that, Elsie?' asked Herbert. 'It's not easy getting the lighting just right.'

'I'll do my best, Herbert,' said Elsie. 'I like to be busy. It keeps me young.'

Sunny said that this sounded like a very good

arrangement and that, although they would miss having Abigail in the shop, he could see that she was needed at the Hotel Splendid.

Ana's mum interrupted Sunny's conversation with the ghosts to say, 'Ana's had a lovely time playing this "haunted hotel" game with you, Sunny.'

'I'm going to miss this place,' said Ana.

'Well,' said her mum, picking up her suitcase, 'perhaps we could come back next summer.' Ana said that would be brilliant, and the ghosts agreed. Ana wheeled her suitcase to the door, turned to wave goodbye and headed out into the sunshine.

Sunny's parents paid their bill and thanked Mrs Griffin, then picked up their luggage and went with Sunny, Herbert, Walter and Violet to the van which was parked outside. When everyone was in and they were about to set off, Sunny saw Mary, Elsie, Abigail and Alan standing in the doorway of the Hotel Splendid, waving them off, and Sunny waved and waved and waved until the hotel and its ghosts were out of sight.

Epilogue

A FEW WEEKS later, a postcard was waiting for Sunny when he got home from his after-school football club. It was signed *with love from Elsie, Mary, Abigail and Alan.*

On the front of the postcard, there was a new photograph of the Hotel Splendid, whose exterior had been repainted and whose missing letters had been replaced. Sunny's mum said how smart it was looking.

Sunny read the message on the back, which explained how the ghosts had fixed the letters: *Alan stood on Abigail's shoulders,* wrote Elsie, *and Abigail stood on Mary's shoulders, and Mary stood on my shoulders. It was possible because we weigh nothing at all, although balancing was tricky, and the 'T' in 'HOTEL' was not easy for Alan to reach, but he managed it. Now the hotel really is splendid – don't you think so?*

Sunny did think so.

The hotel is always full of guests, wrote Elsie. *I have plenty to do on the reception desk, as well as in the dining room. We give a matinee performance every day, and Abigail continues to get rave reviews. Also, my afternoon tea is very popular. Although Mrs Griffin cannot see us, she seems to believe in us now, and enjoys taking afternoon tea with her visitors.*

Sunny's mum put three plates of egg and chips on the table and said, 'What sauces does everyone want?'

'Ketchup, please,' said Sunny.

'Brown sauce, please,' said Sunny's dad. 'What drinks does everyone want?'

'Orange, please,' said Sunny.

'Blackcurrant, please,' said Sunny's mum.

Alan knows lots of interesting local places, wrote Elsie, *which we are looking forward to visiting. The four of us have become very good friends.*

The sauces and the drinks were placed on the table, and Sunny's mum said, 'Right, have we all got what we want?'

Sunny's dad, sitting down, said, 'I think so.'

Sunny propped the postcard against the pepper pot and picked up his knife and fork. 'Yes,' he said, looking at the Hotel Splendid, in front of which he could see four ghosts, arm in arm, smiling and waving. 'I think we have.'

An interview with Abigail Noggle

Up-and-coming actor Abigail Noggle landed her first starring role this summer. She is performing daily in a new play at a popular Devon seaside resort, but made time to answer a few questions.

The ghost that haunts the Hotel Splendid is your first big role. How did you prepare for the part?

I was born to play this role, darling. I'm very grateful to the director, Ana Sharma, for seeing my potential and giving me this opportunity. Ana worked closely with me during the rehearsal process, giving me advice and encouragement. Many performers have a lucky charm or ritual – putting on lucky socks or eating a lucky shepherd's pie before going on stage. Before each performance, I like to do a lucky scream.

What's your favourite colour?

Purple.

Critics have described your performance as 'spooky' and 'mournful', yet in real life you seem to be a very down-to-earth and cheerful person.

When I'm in character, I am the ghost that haunts the Hotel Splendid. I have the most wonderful supporting cast and technical crew who help to create that eerie atmosphere. But when the performance is over, I'm just plain old Abigail Noggle again. I'm not the sort of person who craves attention and praise – I'm perfectly happy hanging out with my friends, just relaxing in between my acclaimed performances in the most successful show on the promenade.

Cats or dogs?

Dogs.

You've received national recognition for your per-formance. What's next? Do you have any ambitions?

It was a lifelong ambition of mine to appear in the West End or on Broadway. I'm always open to new experiences and fresh challenges.

What was your favourite pizza topping?

Sausage and pineapple.

Coming soon!

Sunny and the Wicked Lady

A notoriously scary ghost is supposed to haunt the ruined medieval castle where Sunny and his friends are spending the day. But when a troubling visitor arrives at the antique shop, it turns out the danger is closer to home than they thought . . .

This book has been typeset by
SALT PUBLISHING LIMITED
using Neacademia, a font designed by Sergei Egorov
for the Rosetta Type Foundry in the Czech Republic. It
is manufactured using Holmen Book Cream 70gsm, a
Forest Stewardship Council™ certified paper from the
Hallsta Paper Mill in Sweden. It was printed and bound
by Clays Limited in Bungay, Suffolk, Great Britain.

CROMER
GREAT BRITAIN
MMXIX